GARETH GUIDES TO AN **EXTRAORDINARY** LIFE

Gareth's Guide to

BUILDING A SPACE PROBE

BY THERESE M. SHEA

Gareth Stevens PUBLISHING

Please visit our website, www.garethstevens.com. For a free color catalog of all our high-quality books, call toll free 1-800-542-2595 or fax 1-877-542-2596.

Cataloging-in-Publication Data

Names: Shea, Therese M.
Title: Gareth's guide to building a space probe / Therese M. Shea.
Description: New York : Gareth Stevens Publishing, 2018. | Series: Gareth guides to an extraordinary life | Includes index.
Identifiers: ISBN 9781538203644 (pbk.) | ISBN 9781538203583 (library bound) | ISBN 9781538203378 (6 pack)
Subjects: LCSH: Space probes–Juvenile literature. | Outer space–Exploration–Juvenile literature.
Classification: LCC TL795.3 S44 2018 | DDC 629.43'54–dc23

First Edition

Published in 2018 by
Gareth Stevens Publishing
111 East 14th Street, Suite 349
New York, NY 10003

Editor: Therese Shea

Photo credits: Cover, pp. 1, 15, 21, 25 courtesy of NASA; cover, pp. 1–32 (background texture) Thiti Saichua/Shutterstock.com; cover, pp. 1–32 (design elements) VDOVINA ELENA/Shutterstock.com; p. 5 (main) Nyq/Wikipedia.org; p. 5 (inset) PhilipTerryGraham/Wikipedia.org; p. 6 Mirecki/Wikipedia.org; p. 7 Bricktop/Wikipedia.org; p. 8 Doug Ellison/NASA; p. 9 SimonOrJ/Wikipedia.org; p. 11 NASA/KIM SHIFLETT; p. 13 Alan Mak/Maksim/Wikipedia.org; p. 14 NASA/JPL-Caltech/Alexis Drake; p. 17 NASA/Wikipedia.org; p. 19 (top) HalloweenNight/Wikipedia.org; p. 19 (bottom) PlanetUser/Wikipedia.org; p. 23 Stocktrek Images/Getty Images; p. 27 Kevin Gill (https://www.flickr.com/people/53460575@N03) from Nashua, NH, United States/Wikipedia.org; p. 29 Olaf Frohn/Creative Commons AttributionShareAlike 3.0 Unported License.

Printed in the United States of America

CPSIA compliance information: Batch #CS17GS: For further information contact Gareth Stevens, New York, New York at 1-800-542-2595.

CONTENTS

WORDS IN THE GLOSSARY APPEAR IN **BOLD** TYPE THE FIRST TIME THEY ARE USED IN THE TEXT.

JUNO GOES TO JUPITER

The *Juno* spacecraft launched on August 5, 2011, from Cape Canaveral, Florida. Named for the Roman queen of the gods, *Juno* was programmed to study the fifth planet from the sun, named Jupiter after the Roman king of the gods. But first, it had to get there.

Juno's Atlas rocket provided it with enough speed to reach the **asteroid belt**, but then the sun's gravity pulled it back toward the inner solar system. NASA (National Aeronautics and Space Administration) planned for this in an inventive way. *Juno* would fly by Earth, using Earth's gravity to increase its speed so it could reach Jupiter. This "gravity assist" worked! *Juno* arrived at Jupiter after a 5-year journey on July 4, 2016. NASA had created another successful space probe.

Do you have what it takes to build a space probe?

2,600 MILES (4,200 KM) ← the closest Juno came to Jupiter

SPOTLIGHT!

SCOTT BOLTON, A SCIENTIST WORKING ON THE *JUNO* MISSION, SAID: "WE ARE IN AN ORBIT NOBODY HAS EVER BEEN IN BEFORE, AND THESE IMAGES GIVE US A WHOLE NEW PERSPECTIVE [VIEWPOINT] ON THIS GAS-GIANT WORLD."

Juno's Mission

How much can an unmanned spacecraft tell you about a planet? Scientists are expecting the information from *Juno* will help them discover more about Jupiter's origin! Check out *Juno*'s mission:

- determine the amount of water in Jupiter's atmosphere to test planet formation theories
- measure composition, temperature, and clouds of Jupiter's atmosphere
- explore and study Jupiter's magnetic force field near the planet's poles
- map Jupiter's magnetic and gravity fields

The closest Earth comes to Jupiter is 365 million miles (587 million km). *Juno* has supplied information we could never discover by studying Jupiter from Earth.

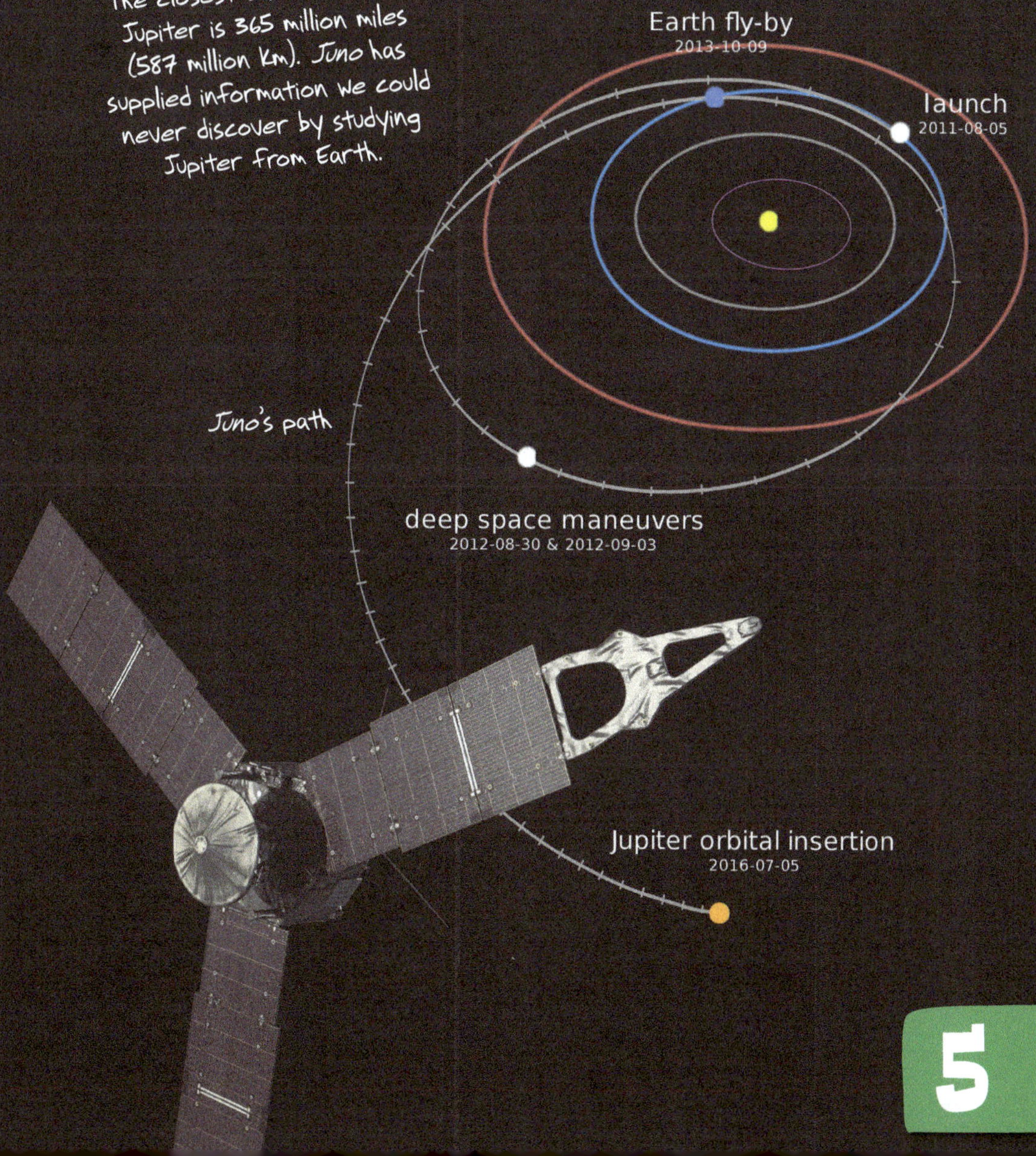

PROBING SPACE PROBES

First, you might ask: "What, exactly, *is* a space probe?" It's any unmanned craft that travels through space to collect information and send it back to Earth for study. It does this using many scientific devices on board that are programmed to gather facts about celestial bodies, such as planets, moons, asteroids, and comets.

There are different kinds of space probes. Orbiters are sent to orbit, or circle, a space body. Landers settle on a surface to collect information. They may carry rovers, which are vehicles that can move around on a surface. Probe missions sometimes plan for craft to fly by a celestial body—or even crash into it in order to gather data! Most probes are designed for a one-way journey, but some do return to Earth.

Stardust space probe

The Stardust Mission

Launched in 1999, *Stardust* was the first space probe to study the composition of a comet. It gathered space dust in 2000 and 2002 with the help of an instrument called an aerogel collector. It worked like a sponge; particles hit it and got stuck inside. In 2004, the probe flew by a comet called Wild 2. It got close enough to catch particles streaming from the comet. These particles were returned to Earth in 2006.

Among the exciting results of studying the bits of dust captured by *Stardust's* aerogel collector was the discovery of an **amino acid** called glycine, one of the building blocks of life.

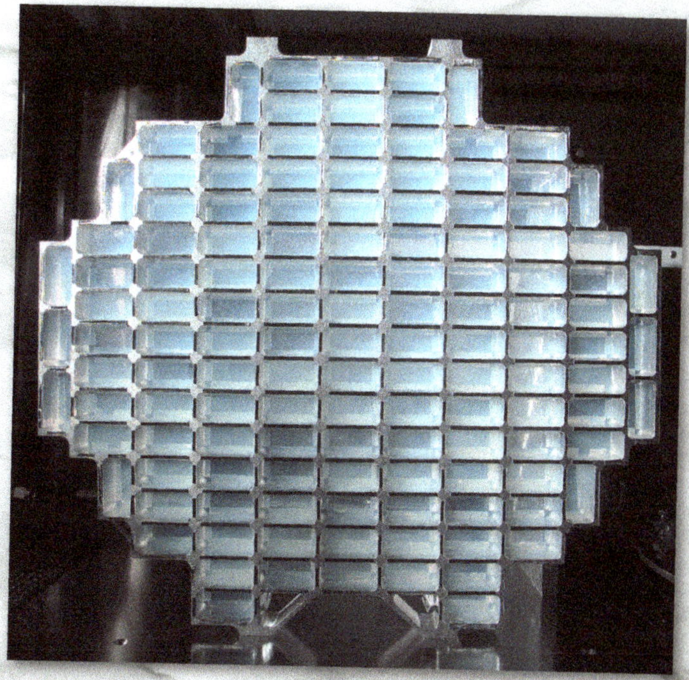

3,200,000,000 MILES (5,100,000,000 KM) → *Stardust's* total journey

SPOTLIGHT!

THE AEROGEL SUBSTANCE USED BY *STARDUST* TO COLLECT COMET PARTICLES IS LISTED IN GUINNESS WORLD RECORDS AS THE LIGHTEST KNOWN SOLID MATERIAL!

Space probes transmit data back to Earth using radio waves. Each craft has a transmitter as well as a receiver. Onboard **technology** interprets the radio waves it receives from Earth as commands.

Just as radio waves on Earth get weaker the farther we are from the source, radio waves can get very, very faint as they travel great distances across the solar system. That's why NASA and other space agencies use large and carefully aimed radio receivers to send and collect radio signals. The NASA Deep Space Network—or DSN—is a system of antennas around the world that aids with this communication. It's the biggest and most sensitive scientific communications system on Earth.

SPOTLIGHT!

THE LARGEST AND MOST SENSITIVE OF DSN'S ANTENNAS CAN TRACK SPACECRAFT MORE THAN 10 BILLION MILES (16 BILLION KM) FROM EARTH.

This DSN antenna in California is 230 feet (70 m) wide. Each of the three DSN facilities has an antenna this size for the farthest communications.

The DSN

The DSN is made up of three communications facilities equally spaced around the world, each about one-third of the way around Earth. One is at Goldstone, near Barstow, California, in the Mojave Desert. Another is positioned near Madrid, Spain, and the last is close to Canberra in Australia. These locations mean at least one station is always at the right position to send signals to and receive signals from a space probe or other craft.

A space probe must be 18,600 miles (30,000 km) from Earth before it's always in the path of one of the DSN communications facilities.

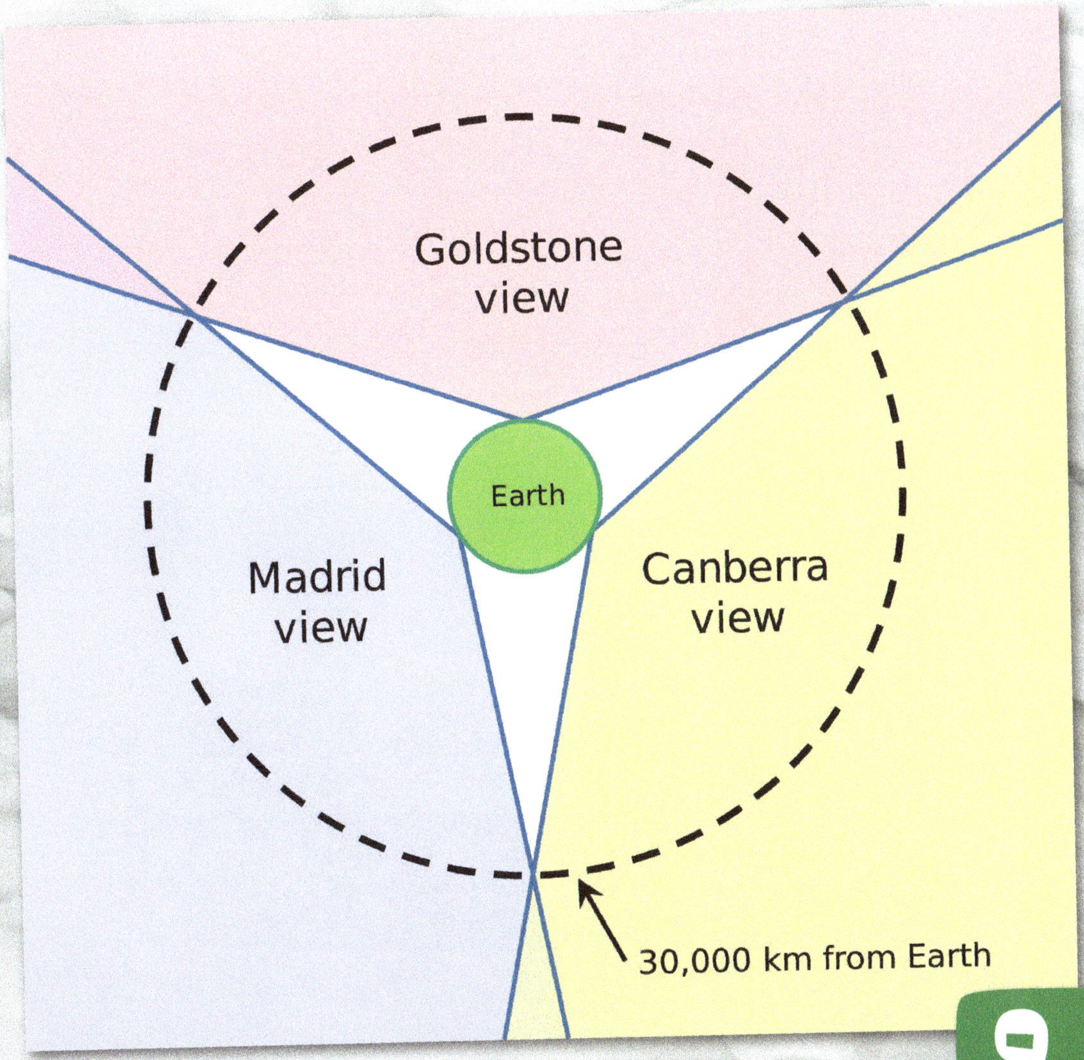

WORKING IN AEROSPACE

Sure, you could try building a space probe yourself now, but you might have more success if you went to school to become an aerospace engineer first. An aerospace engineer is concerned with designing, building, testing, and operating vehicles in Earth's atmosphere and beyond: the aerospace.

If this seems like a lot of work, it is! That's why teams of engineers work together on large projects. They concentrate on specific tasks, check and double-check each other's work, and share the satisfaction of seeing their vehicle soar into space.

Most aerospace engineers work for the government or for businesses that build craft for the government. But if you want to be an aerospace engineer who builds a space probe, you might want to work for NASA.

SPOTLIGHT!

NEIL ARMSTRONG, THE FIRST MAN ON THE MOON, WAS AN AEROSPACE ENGINEER. HE ONCE SAID: "I AM, AND EVER WILL BE, A WHITE-SOCKS, POCKET-PROTECTOR, NERDY ENGINEER."

NASA

US Congress created NASA in 1958 with an act to build a national space program. NASA has many functions: to research problems concerning flight within and outside Earth's atmosphere; to develop, build, test, and operate space vehicles; to explore space with manned and unmanned vehicles; to work with other countries on space projects; and to publish the results of its work for the public. NASA needs engineers, writers, scientists, and anyone who's interested in space exploration!

Aerospace engineers are sometimes called rocket scientists, but that's not accurate. They work on many more parts of spacecraft than the rockets that propel them, or move them forward.

THE JET PROPULSION LABORATORY

Where are space probes built? In the United States, the Jet Propulsion Laboratory, or the JPL, is the center for robotic exploration in the solar system. Though it's a part of NASA today, it was building spacecraft before NASA existed. It's based in Pasadena, California, and managed by the California Institute of Technology.

The JPL doesn't just construct space probes. It also develops **satellites**, runs the Deep Space Network, and manages space telescopes and **observatories**. Almost all US unmanned space missions have been planned, designed, built, and operated by the JPL.

NASA has other research centers, too, including Ames Research Center in Moffett Field, California; Langley Research Center in Hampton, Virginia; and Glenn Research Center in Cleveland, Ohio.

5,000 → number of JPL employees

SPOTLIGHT!

AN OBSERVATORY ON TABLE MOUNTAIN, CALIFORNIA, IS AN IDEAL LOCATION FOR OBSERVING THE NIGHT SKIES, WHICH IS WHY IT, TOO, IS A PART OF THE JPL.

Other Space Agencies

NASA isn't the only organization sending probes into space. Other agencies include the European Space Agency (ESA), the Russian Federal Space Agency (ROSCOSMOS), the Canadian Space Agency (CSA), and the Japan Aerospace Exploration Agency (JAXA). These organizations and others sometimes work together on missions, including the space station orbiting Earth called the International Space Station, or ISS. Scientists from these and other countries do important research aboard the ISS.

There's a tradition in the JPL control room where employees send data to and receive data from probes. They pass around peanuts to bring the mission good luck!

To get a job at the JPL, you can have any kind of background. The JPL needs people who can write well, do math, and understand a variety of computer languages. However, if you want to work on developing and building a space probe, you should study related fields such as chemistry, physics, mathematics, and engineering, especially robotics and aerospace engineering. Graduating college is a must, but graduate school is important to gain in-depth knowledge. Students can join organizations such as robotics and astronomy clubs to practice their skills.

You might not even have to wait until you graduate from college to work at the JPL. It offers special jobs for students, **internships**, and career opportunities for new graduates as well. Check out the different kinds of positions on the JPL website: www.jpl.nasa.gov/opportunities/.

SPOTLIGHT!

ONE STUDENT WHO WAS AWARDED A SUMMER INTERNSHIP WITH THE JPL SAID SHE BEGAN COLLEGE WITHOUT A CAREER IN MIND: "GETTING INTO STEM [SCIENCE, TECHNOLOGY, ENGINEERING, AND MATH] REALLY SAVED ME, AND HELPED ME FOCUS MY DIRECTION AND GOALS."

Collecting Space Dust

You might work on a space probe while studying about them! Students at the University of Colorado majoring in physics, mechanical engineering, aeronautics, and other sciences were selected to build a space dust collector for the *New Horizons* space probe. Its purpose is to study space dust on the probe's journey to the dwarf planet Pluto. The device is called the Venetia Burney Student Dust Counter (VBSDC), after the 11-year-old girl who named Pluto.

VBSDC scientist Dr. David James said: "If you were an alien world looking into our solar system and saw all the dust, what you'd really be looking at is the footprints of our planets. . . .They can tell us what used to be there."

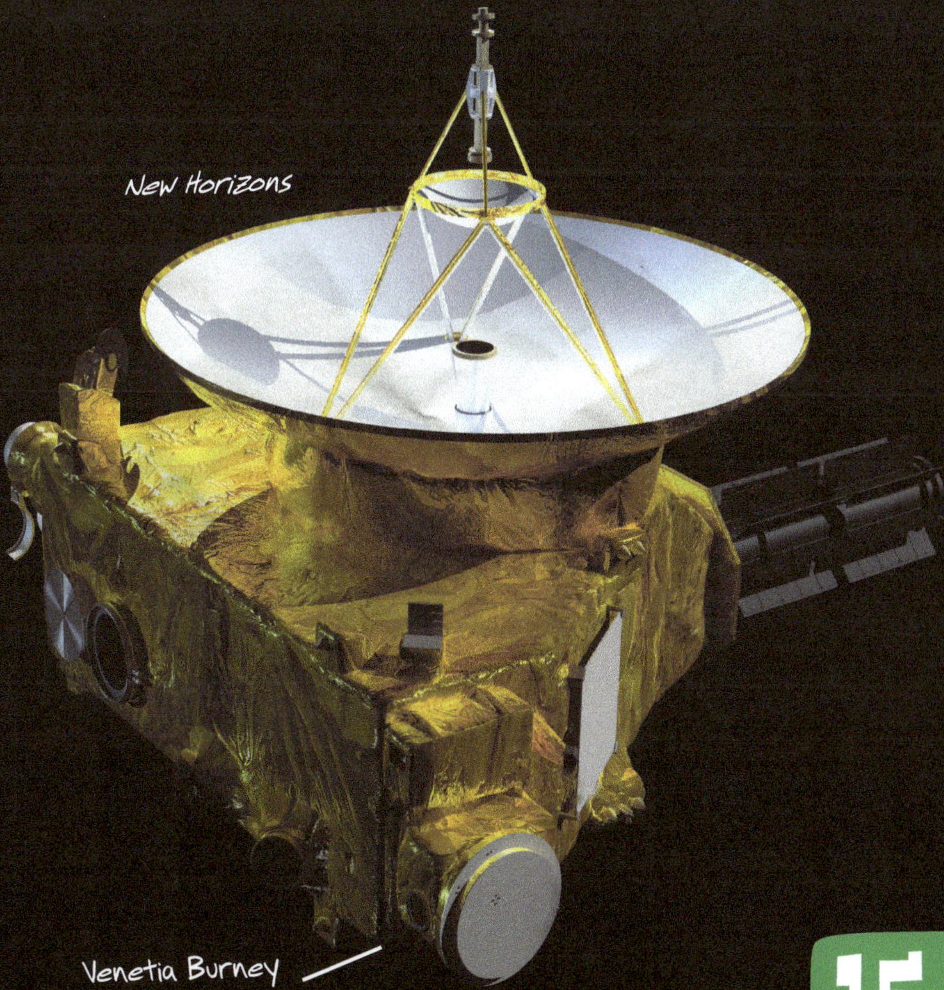

TIME TO DESIGN

Let's fast-forward a few years. You've been to high school, college, and graduate school. You're an aerospace technology genius, and NASA has hired you to build their next probe at the JPL. How do you start?

All probes need to be designed with certain things in mind:

1. solar **radiation**–Energy from the sun can damage computers and other electrical systems; special shields can protect technology from radiation.
2. temperature–Probes traveling closer to the sun need cooling systems; those traveling away need heating systems. Most probes need both!
3. power source–Probes run on electricity, which needs a power source such as solar cells (most effective near the sun) or nuclear energy (for travel farther from the sun).

43 YEARS AND 13 BILLION MILES (21 BILLION KM) FROM EARTH → expected life of the *Voyager 1* probe's nuclear batteries

SPOTLIGHT!

PLANETS WITH STRONG MAGNETIC FIELDS, SUCH AS JUPITER, ALSO HAVE STRONG RADIATION BELTS THAT CAN HARM PROBES.

Battling the Sun

Radiation shielding is heavy and expensive, so engineers often look for other ways of dealing with the sun's energy. Sometimes engineers use special "radiation-hardened" electronics. These can be costly, too. Another approach is to use three systems to figure out the same thing. If one of the systems makes an error because of radiation, the other two should arrive at the right answer.

New Horizons flew by the dwarf planet Pluto in 2015. This probe is covered in a gold film that retains heat far from the sun. It has radiation-hardened electronics as well.

4. driving force–The probe needs something to propel it. Most probes use rockets propelled by chemical reactions, while some use electrical energy. The probe's path can make use of planetary gravity, as *Juno* did.
5. communication system–Antennas are sufficient closer to Earth, but most distant probes need large radio dishes to catch signals.

Besides these factors, you must also consider where the probe will be traveling. If its destination is a planet, what will the weather be like on the planet? Neptune's winds whip as fast as 1,200 miles (1,930 km) per hour. If your space probe is headed there, it would need to be able to stand up to such winds.

SPOTLIGHT!

ON AUGUST 6, 2013, *CURIOSITY* PLAYED THE "HAPPY BIRTHDAY" SONG IN HONOR OF EXPLORING MARS FOR 1 EARTH YEAR. THIS WAS THE FIRST TIME A SONG WAS PLAYED ON ANOTHER PLANET!

365 EARTH DAYS → length of 1 Earth year

687 EARTH DAYS → length of 1 Mars year

Rovers

Some lander probes sent to Mars have carried electrical-powered vehicles called rovers. They're semiautonomous, which means they're partially able to make decisions about their actions. However, they do receive radio communications from Earth, too. The Mars rover *Opportunity* landed on Mars in 2004 for a 90-day mission, but it's still exploring! The rover *Curiosity* landed in 2012 and has been acting as a geology lab on Mars ever since. It has discovered that Mars once had conditions that could have supported life.

The *Ulysses* probe, shown below, was sent to study the sun. You can see the high-gain antenna here. The amount of gain refers to the amount of incoming radio power the antenna can collect.

Even if you design and build a space probe that can make the journey, don't forget that you're sending it out for a purpose. Here are some past missions of space probes:

- map the surface of a planet or moon, and measure geographic features such as mountains and valleys
- measure climate, such as surface temperature and wind speed
- discover what a space object's atmosphere is composed of
- investigate the composition of a space object's surface
- collect samples of matter from space objects

You must equip your probe with tools to fulfill these missions. Special instruments can be fitted to a probe to fulfill these tasks. They must be sturdy enough to make the journey, work with the probe's computers, and provide data that can be transmitted back to Earth.

7-10 YEARS

mission length of NASA's lunar probes

SPOTLIGHT!

OUR MOON ONCE HAD A MAGNETIC FIELD, AS EARTH DOES. WE KNOW THIS FROM MOON ROCKS BROUGHT BACK BY THE *APOLLO 11* MISSION. TWO NASA PROBES HAVE BEEN STUDYING THE MOON SINCE 2011.

Space Tech Tools

Scientific instruments on space probes include cameras to take photographs; some kinds can also detect temperatures. Magnetometers can measure magnetic fields. Radar is another useful instrument that uses radio waves to locate objects, determine distance, and even map the landscape. Spectrometers are instruments that can split light into its different wavelengths. Measuring these wavelengths can help scientists identify the composition of space objects. If the probe includes a lander, the lander may have shovels or drills to collect samples.

Check out *Juno's* payload, a term that means all the equipment (and sometimes, people) carried by a spacecraft.

MATERIALS TO BUILD

Now you know what you want to build. What materials will you need to build it? Most spacecraft are built with strong, lightweight metals, such as aluminum, magnesium, and titanium. These metals can withstand great heat and pressure such as the conditions the craft's **bulkhead** encounters during launch and in Earth's atmosphere.

Engineers are always testing new materials that could lower the weight of spacecraft such as superthin films called gossamer materials. Carbon **composites** (like those found in tennis rackets and golf clubs) are already used. A new material called the carbon nanotube isn't just lightweight, it's much, much stronger than steel! Scientists are hoping to be able to manufacture this amazing substance.

600 TIMES

how much stronger carbon nanotubes are than steel

SPOTLIGHT!

GALACTIC COSMIC RADIATION (GCR) MOSTLY ORIGINATES OUTSIDE OUR SOLAR SYSTEM. IT CAN SPLIT THE NUCLEUS OF A METAL'S ATOMS!

Fantastic Plastic

Plastic is a material that may cover manned and unmanned spacecraft someday. Because it's rich in hydrogen, it's effective in blocking high-energy radiation—cosmic rays—that can cause cancer and even destroy DNA bonds. "It turns out that the worst materials you can use for shielding against [galactic cosmic radiation] are metals," said Dennis Bushnell, chief scientist at Langley Research Center.

Spacecraft may need parachutes for slowing down before a landing. Parachutes can be made of familiar fabrics such as polyester and nylon. The rope connecting them to the vehicle is often made of Kevlar, a material used in bulletproof vests!

ON THE LAUNCHPAD

Your probe is ready for space exploration. The last step is getting it out there, and that's challenging. Escape **velocity** is the minimum velocity that a moving object must have to escape from the gravitational field of a celestial body and move outward into space. A spacecraft leaving Earth needs to be going about 7 miles (11 km) per second, or over 25,000 miles (40,200 km) per hour, to enter orbit. All probes are currently launched using chemical rockets.

Chemical rocket engines use a fuel and an oxidizer–a type of chemical that must be present in order for fuel to burn. The chemical reaction produces rapidly expanding hot gases. These are ejected at high speed from the rocket, creating enough thrust to shoot the craft beyond the pull of Earth's gravity.

SPOTLIGHT!

A SPACE PROBE IS SURROUNDED BY A CASING TO AVOID DAMAGE DURING LAUNCH. THE ROCKET AND CASING FALL AWAY AS THE PROBE MAKES ITS JOURNEY.

Ion Thrusters

Ion thrusters are a newer way of moving deep-space vehicles. An ion is an atom or molecule that has an electrical charge because it's lost or gained an electron. Ionization is the process of giving a charge to an atom or a molecule by adding or removing electrons. Once charged, ions can be moved by magnetism. Ion propulsion systems use this reaction to generate a tiny amount of thrust for propulsion. They can do this over a long period of time. Ion thrusters may eventually propel spacecraft 200,000 miles (320,000 km) per hour.

The space probe *OSIRIS-REx* lifted off from Cape Canaveral, Florida, in 2016 propelled by an Atlas V 411 rocket. Its mission is to study the asteroid 101955 Bennu and return a sample to Earth in 2023.

THINKING OUTSIDE THE BOX

Scientists and engineers are thinking of some clever ways of improving spacecraft. One idea is placing **sensors** into the craft's outer walls, a bit like our skin has nerves that can feel. Currently, sensors are a separate piece of equipment. Perhaps this spacecraft "skin" could even be made of material that could repair damage done to it by bits of comets and asteroids. Substances made up of long-chain molecules called ionomers react to holes by closing up again!

In 2016, famous physicist Stephen Hawking and other scientists announced their endeavor to send a supersmall, superlight probe to nearby star Alpha Centauri. It would be carried by a solar sail and powered by a **laser** beamed from Earth. They expect the journey to take 20 years.

SPOTLIGHT!

"WITH LIGHT BEAMS, LIGHT SAILS, AND THE LIGHTEST SPACECRAFT EVER BUILT, WE CAN LAUNCH A MISSION TO ALPHA CENTAURI WITHIN A GENERATION," STEPHEN HAWKING SAID. "TODAY, WE COMMIT TO THIS NEXT GREAT LEAP INTO THE COSMOS. BECAUSE WE ARE HUMAN, AND OUR NATURE IS TO FLY."

Solar Sail

A solar sail (also called a light sail) is a giant sail, somewhat like the piece of fabric that moves a sailboat. However, it's made of a superthin, reflective material and propelled by radiation! In 2010, the Japan Aerospace Exploration Agency used a solar sail to drive its probe IKAROS (Interplanetary Kite-craft Accelerated by Radiation Of the Sun). It flew by Venus 6 months later and was considered a success.

It's essential that the payload attached to a solar sail be very light.

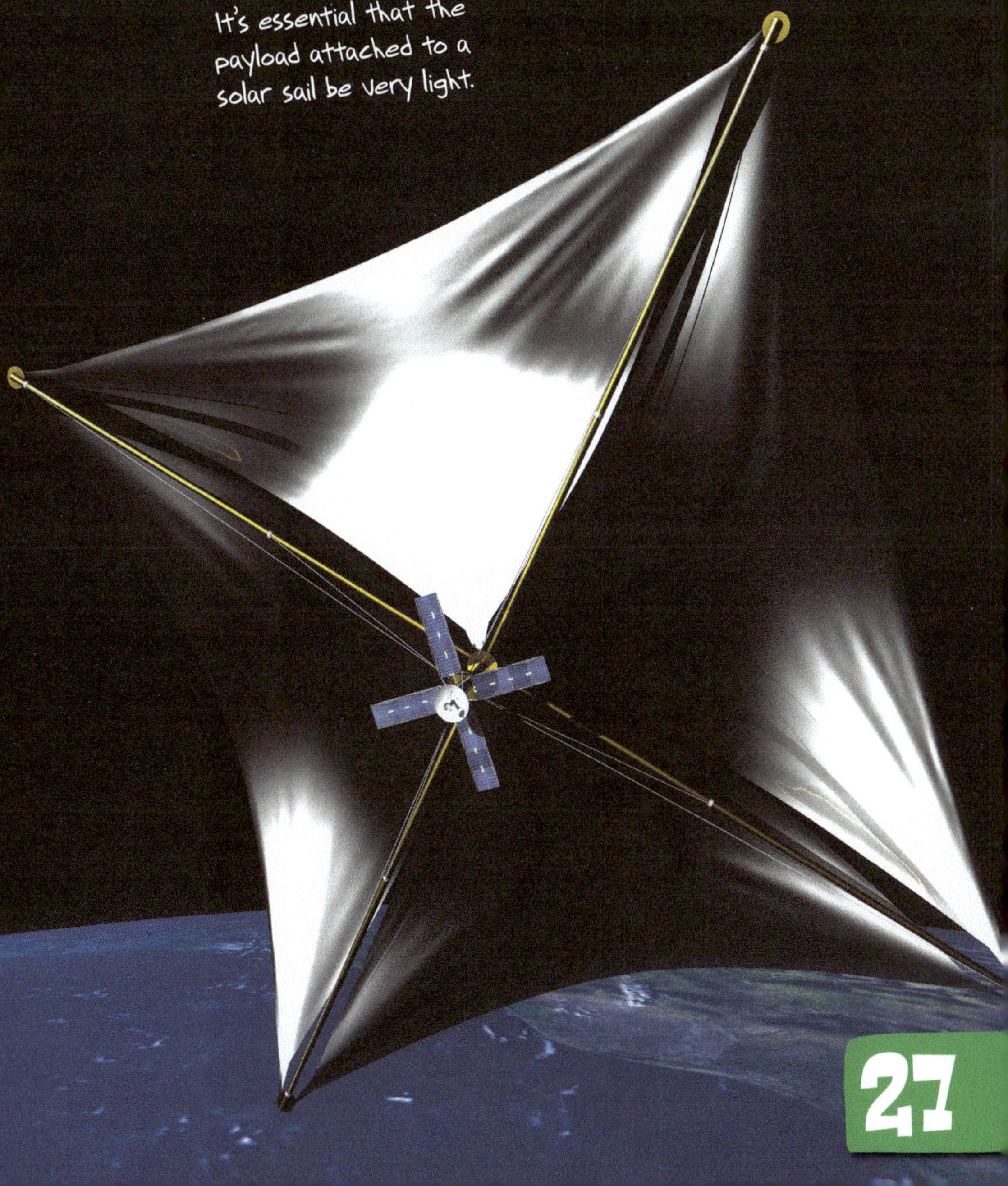

WHY WE EXPLORE

Space probes are expensive: the *Juno* mission to Jupiter cost over $1 billion! The US government funds NASA with tax money. Space.com estimates that about half a penny of every federal tax dollar ends up at NASA, though funding has been cut over the years. Sometimes, people wonder if space exploration is worth the cost. Money could be spent in other areas of need.

Other people point out that space has always been of interest to humans, and now we have the technology to explore it. We know that planets and moons have natural resources that could be of use to us on Earth. Space may also offer us another home someday. So far, space probes offer us the best chance to understand our solar system–and beyond!

TIPS FOR BUILDING A SPACE PROBE:

> Study aerospace engineering or a similar field.
> Work for NASA's Jet Propulsion Laboratory.
> Collaborate with a team of experts.
> Decide what kind of probe you will make.
> Decide where it will travel and what it will study.
> Use strong, lightweight materials in its construction.
> Equip it with radiation-hardened scientific devices.
> Launch it using a chemical rocket.
> Communicate with it using the Deep Space Network.

Weight Is Money

A report estimates that each pound of a spacecraft costs about $5,000 to launch into space. That's why it's so important to reduce the weight of spacecraft. However, parts and materials can't just be removed or replaced without considering how the absence of the material and the addition of another, lighter material will affect the safety of the object or the likelihood of it achieving its mission.

SPOT A SPACE PROBE

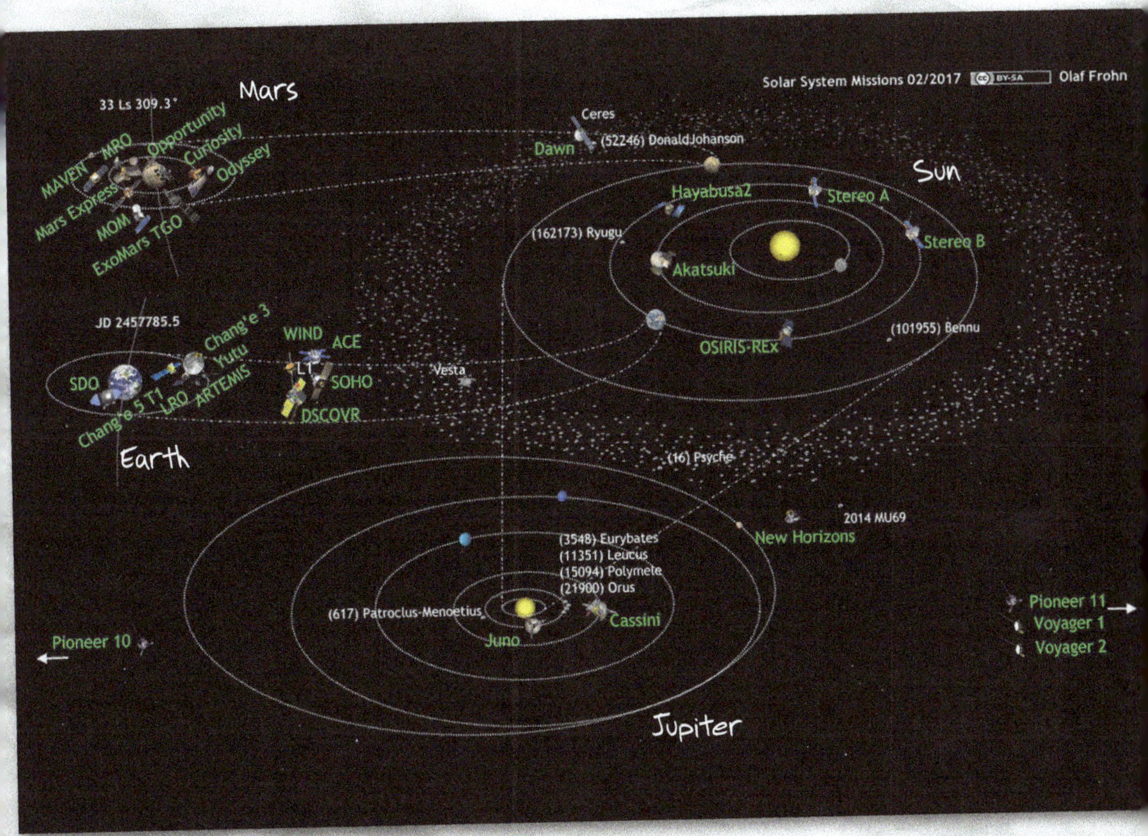

Here are the locations of space probes around the solar system as of January 2017.

GLOSSARY

amino acid: any one of many acids that occur naturally in living things and that include some which form proteins

asteroid belt: the region of interplanetary space between the orbits of Mars and Jupiter in which most asteroids are found

bulkhead: a wall that separates the different parts of a ship or aircraft

composite: something that is made up of different parts

internship: a job for a period of time for the purpose of gaining experience

laser: a device that produces a narrow and powerful beam of light

observatory: a special building for studying stars, planets, or weather

radiation: energy that comes from a source in the form of waves or rays you cannot see and that can be dangerous

satellite: a machine that is sent into space and that moves around Earth, the moon, or a planet

sensor: a device that detects or senses heat, light, sound, or motion and then reacts to it in a particular way

technology: a machine, piece of equipment, or method that is useful in solving a problem

velocity: the rate of change in the position of an object in a certain direction

FOR MORE INFORMATION

Books

Couper, Heather, and Nigel Henbest. *DK Encyclopedia of Space*. New York, NY: DK Publishing, 2009.

Kortenkamp, Steve. *Future Explorers: Robots in Space*. North Mankato, MN: Capstone Press, 2016.

Sparrow, Giles. *Space Exploration*. Mankato, MN: Smart Apple Media, 2012.

Websites

Careers in Aerospace Technology
www.nasa.gov/centers/langley/news/factsheets/FS-2001-09-68-LaRC.html
Find out if you have the right stuff for a career at NASA.

Missions
www.jpl.nasa.gov/missions/
Read about the many NASA space probe missions.

Rockets: Looking Closer
sciencelearn.org.nz/Contexts/Rockets/Looking-Closer
Learn more about rockets in space exploration.

INDEX